A SHARK NAMED

It was just a normal sunny day, deep in the sea at Tiger Beach...

The only difference was Pickles, the tiger shark, woke up extra hungry.

"Wow, I sure am hungry today."

But uh-oh,
Pickles was out of food!

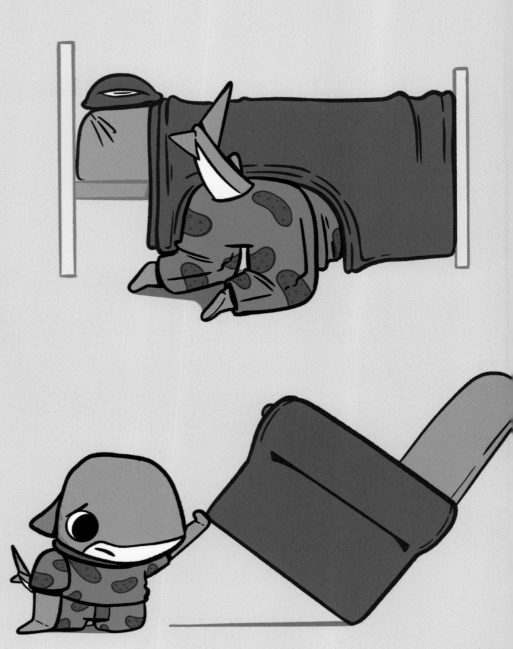

None in the fridge, none in the pantry, none anywhere in her ship!

"Well, I guess I better find something to eat," says Pickles.
And she brushed her teeth, got dressed, and set out to find food.

On her search, Pickles found the most delicious burger and fries outside her favorite cafe!

Then Pickles stopped for a few pieces of candy she spotted at Seaweed park.

She even found a whole box of chicken nuggets and quickly gobbled them up!

By the time Pickles had finished the snack adventure, she was ready for a nap.

But just as Pickles drifted off to sleep, her stomach started grumbling...

And grumbling...

Until it was grumbling so loud she couldn't sleep!

"Hey Pilot! I've got..uhhhghghgh..my tummy is grumbling so loud! I think something might be wrong.. Can you come help?"

"I'll swim right over!" Pilot says and clicks off his shellphone.

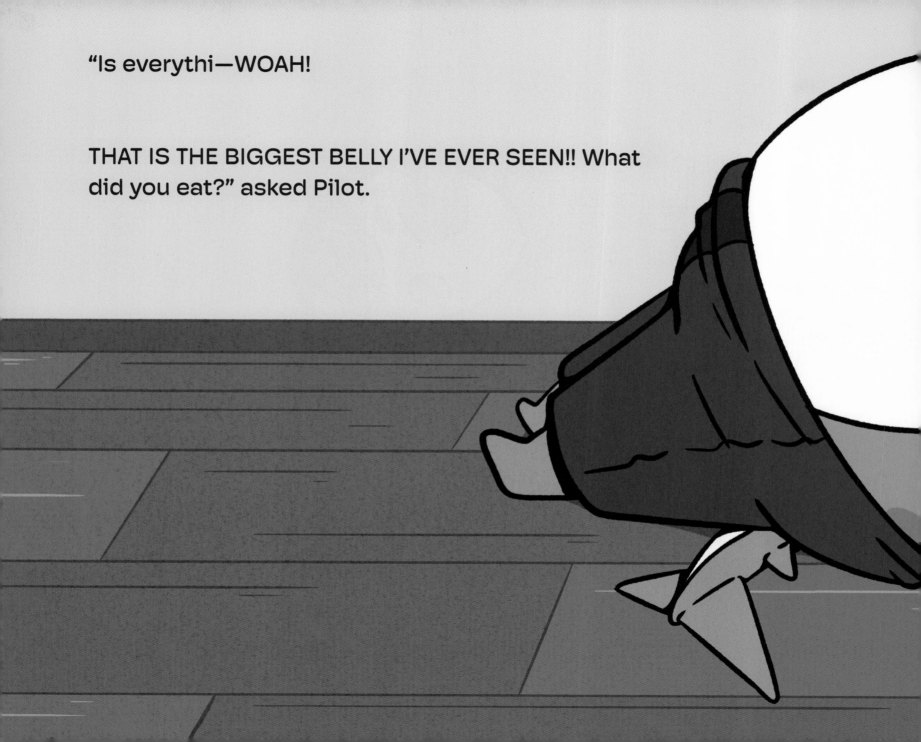

"Is everythi—WOAH!

THAT IS THE BIGGEST BELLY I'VE EVER SEEN!! What did you eat?" asked Pilot.

"Uhh.." Pickles looks down.

"It's okay, Pickles. Let's take a look inside," Pilot says.

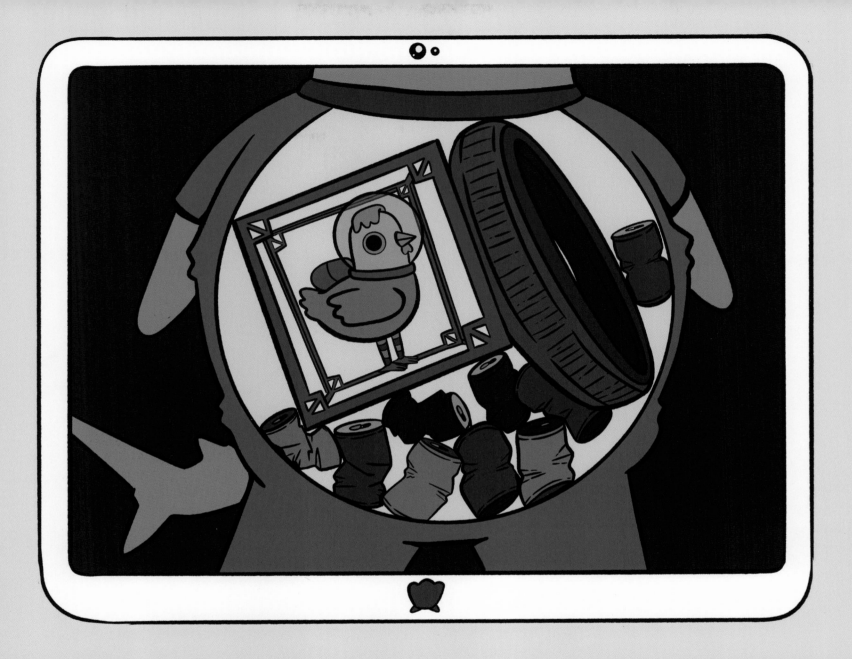

"Wow, Pickles. There is a whole bunch of junk in there... We've got to get it out."

What is that . . ." Pickles asked nervously.

"Relax! It won't hurt a bit!" shouts Pilot.

Pilot reached the tool deep down into Pickles tummy and said, "1... 2... 3!" and gave a big tug. "Pickles.. You ate a TIRE?! Where did this come from?" asked Pilot.

"Well..." Pickles thinks.

Pickles' stomach rumbles again so Pilot wiggles and jiggles the tool into place.

Pilot yanks out a slippery, slimy cluster of cans!

"Huh!? I thought that was candy..." says a puzzled Pickles.

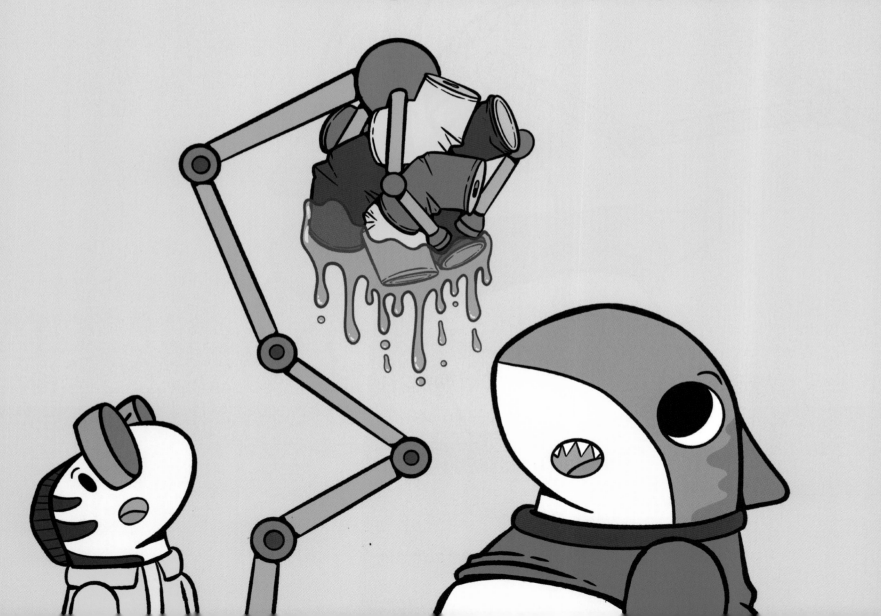

"Okay Pickles, deep breath! Only one more time..."

"CLUCK, CLUUUCK, CLUUUUUUCK!!!" screams Nugget the Chicken as Pilot pulls out a whole chicken coop.

"Goodness, Pickles. How in the world did you eat all this junk?" Pilot asks.

"I found it all over Tiger Beach! I was so hungry and it all looked so good!
Come on, let me show you," Pickles grabs Pilot's fin.

First, they stop by Tiger Beach Cafe where they find car tires and buns. "It does kinda look like a really big burger..." Pilot says.

Then, they stop by the Seaweed Park where Pickles found all the CAN-dy!

And on their way back, Pickles shows Pilot where she found Nugget... and Nugget's friends!

"I was just so hungry!" Pickles says "I thought they were nuggets!"

"Wow, Pickles! There is so much trash. This isn't good for you or the ocean," says Pilot.

"Let's clean all this up, so no other hungry sea creatures accidentally eat trash and get tummy trouble." Pickles suggests.

"Phew! That is so much better!" Pilot says to Pickles as they kick back, relax and enjoy their new, clean beach.

Matt "The Shark Guy" Marchant is a shark author, award winning photographer, and ocean conservationist. Matt has spent years diving with all types of sharks and loves to share his experiences young shark lovers. He lives in Austin, Texas with his wife and kids. Find more of his work at www.learnaboutsharks.com

Ashten Wickham is an illustrator, currently based in the Pacific Northwest. With a keen eye for color and a knack for creating fun and captivating character designs, Ashten brings a playful yet weighted energy to every story he has the honor of illustrating. Discover more of his work at www.ashtenwickham.com

Pickles is an adult female tiger shark. She loves long swims on the beach, eating and being awesome! 🦈

Fedd Books
P.O. Box 341973
Austin, TX 78734

www.thefeddagency.com

Illustrated by Ashten Wickham

Published in association with The Fedd Agency, Inc., a literary agency.

ISBN: 978-1-957616-50-6

LCCN: 2023914713

Printed in the United States of America